TALES FROM MANY LANDS PAPERCRAFTS

Written and illustrated by
Jerome C. Brown

Fearon Teacher Aids
Simon & Schuster Supplementary Education Group

Editor: Carol Williams
Copyeditor: Kristin Eclov
Design: Diann Abbott

ISBN 0-8224-3157-2
Printed in the United States of America

1. 9 8 7 6 5 4 3 2 1

CONTENTS

INTRODUCTION

This book contains directions and patterns for making masks and a variety of puppets to enhance the enjoyment of tales from around the world. Most of the stories can be found in your local library in a book bearing the title's name. "The Lad and the North Wind" is sometimes called "Peter and the North Wind" and can be found in a collection of Norwegian tales. "The Straw Ox" can be found in a collection of Russian tales. Read each tale aloud to your class with expression and enthusiasm before beginning the papercraft projects.

Organizational Helps

Construction paper is used in each papercraft. It is referred to as art paper in the list of materials that accompanies each project. Colors of art paper are suggested but can be changed to suit your needs. Since you will need a pencil, ruler, scissors, glue, and markers or crayons for each project, these items are not listed in each materials list.

For each art project children enjoy, the teacher must spend time in preparation and gathering supplies. This book was designed to minimize that time. A special instruction sheet for making the masks has been included at the beginning of this book. Each mask requires the cutting and tracing of individual pieces on colored art paper. Once students have mastered the basic format, projects will take less time and explanation. Whole sheets [12" x 18" (30.5 cm x 45.7 cm)], half sheets [9" x 12" (22.9 cm x 30.5 cm)], and quarter sheets [6" x 9" (15.2 cm x 22.9 cm)] of art paper are used whenever possible. This will cut down on the time spent measuring and cutting. For younger students, reproduce the pattern pages (eliminating the words on the patterns) on white art paper and have students simply color the pieces before cutting and assembling. Stick puppets are frequently used throughout this book. A special dotted line has been drawn around the figures to make cutting easier for younger children. Older children can ignore the dotted line and cut out the intricate details of the figures.

Uses for Papercrafts

A coloring page is the first activity listed for each story. Invite children to staple the coloring pages together in a book with a sheet of writing paper between each coloring page. Encourage children to write a story summary, a different ending, or rewrite their favorite part of each story following the coloring page. Or, children can research information about the country from which each tale comes and write down some interesting facts.

Plays and skits can be designed around the masks and puppets. Assign different characters to students and group them to create dialogue and practice a reenactment of the tale. Directions for a puppet theatre are given on page 64 and can be used in a variety of ways. Older children may enjoy making the projects and presenting a skit to a younger group of children.

Display the projects on a mural or bulletin board. Invite the students to create a background with chalk or paint.

It is the author's hope that these papercrafts will allow you to bring literature to life in your classroom.

Masks

Fold paper for head and neck lengthwise (fig. A). Use the color of art paper listed on the project page. Trace and cut out two heads and two 1" x 10" (2.5 cm x 25.4 cm) strips (fig. B). Be sure to also trace eye holes. Leave head folded and cut out eye holes. Cut through dotted line to make cutting the small hole easier (fig. C). To make neck, cover 1" x 10" (2.5 cm x 25.4 cm) cardboard strip with art paper strips. Glue neck between the two heads allowing 6" (15.2 cm) to extend (fig. D).

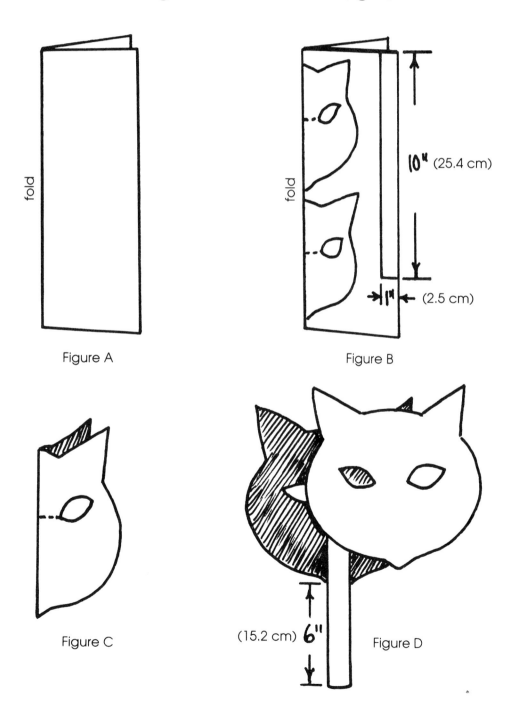

fold

Figure A

fold

10" (25.4 cm)

1" (2.5 cm)

Figure B

Figure C

(15.2 cm) 6"   Figure D

The Bojabi Tree (Africa)

The Bojabi Tree (Robin Rat and King Leo Masks)

Materials

- One 1" x 10" (2.5 cm x 25.4 cm) cardboard strip for each puppet

Art Paper (Robin Rat):

- Gray 12" x 18" (30.5 cm x 45.7 cm) head, neck
- Yellow 6" x 9" (15.2 cm x 22.9 cm) hat
- Red 6" x 9" (15.2 cm x 22.9 cm) hat visor, tassel
- Pink 4 1/2" x 6" (11.4 cm x 15.2 cm) muzzle, inner ears
- Black scrap for nose

Art Paper (King Leo):

- Brown 12" x 18" (30.5 cm x 45.7 cm) head, neck
- Yellow 9" x 12" (22.9 cm x 30.5 cm) mane
- Aluminum foil 3" x 6" (7.6 cm x 15.2 cm) crown
- Black scrap for nose

Procedure

1. Follow directions on page 5 for tracing, cutting, and gluing head and cardboard neck strip.

2. Trace and cut out remaining pattern pieces.

3. Glue pieces in place (figs. A and B).

4. Add details with markers or crayons.

Figure A

Figure B

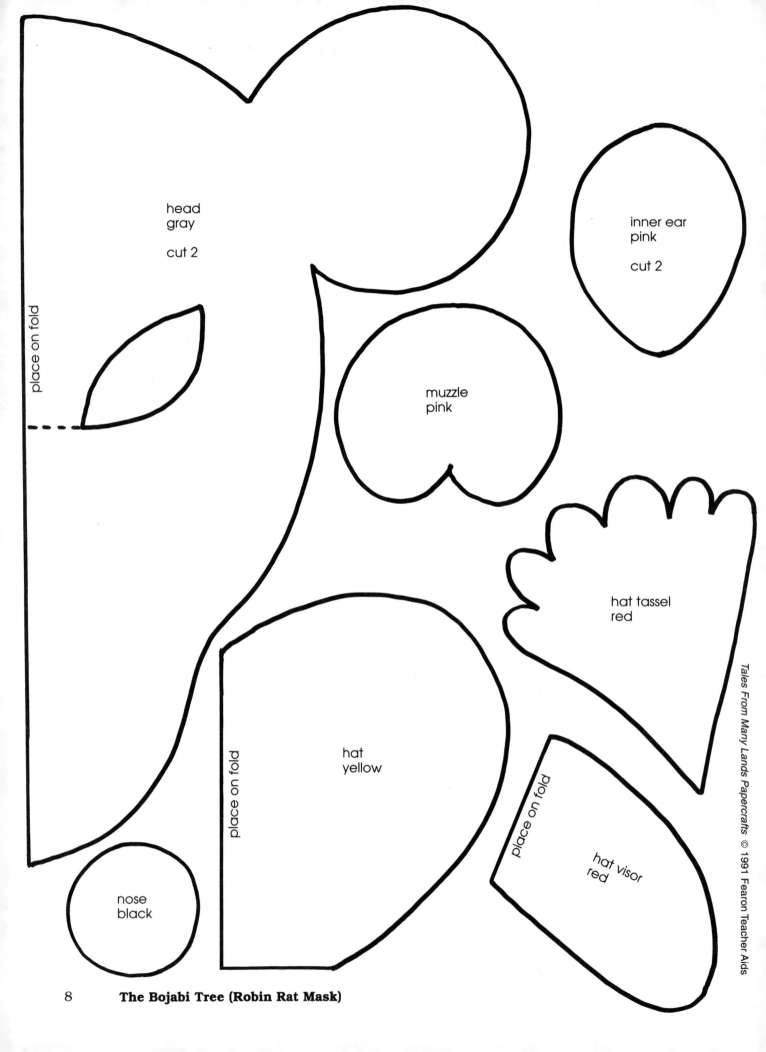

head
gray

cut 2

inner ear
pink

cut 2

place on fold

muzzle
pink

hat tassel
red

hat
yellow

place on fold

place on fold

hat visor
red

nose
black

8   **The Bojabi Tree (Robin Rat Mask)**

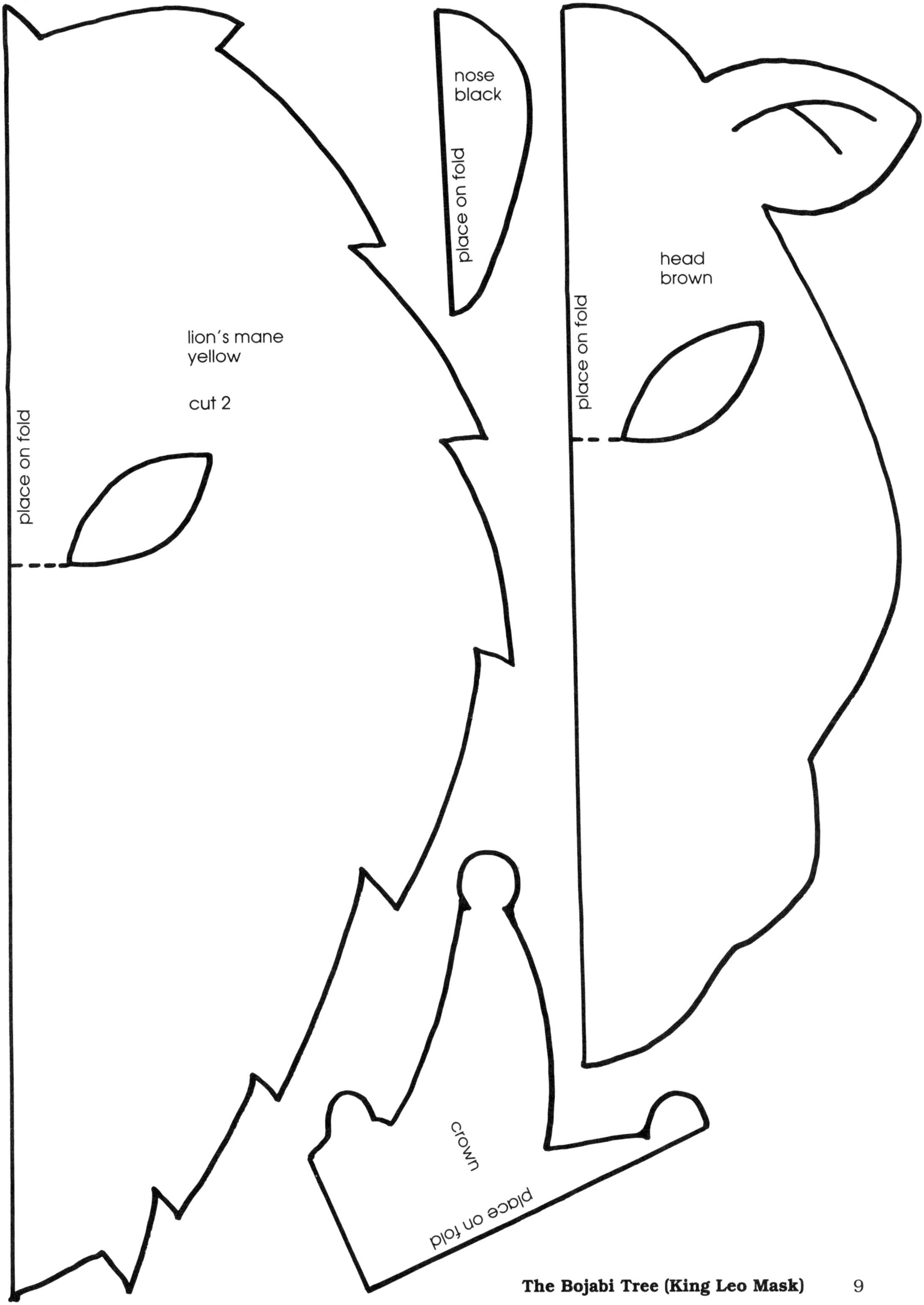

nose
black

place on fold

lion's mane
yellow

cut 2

place on fold

head
brown

place on fold

crown

place on fold

The Bojabi Tree (King Leo Mask) 9

The Bojabi Tree (Pinky Pig, Giddy Goat, and Tommy Tortoise Masks)

Materials

- One 1" x 10" (2.5 cm x 25.4 cm) cardboard strip for each puppet

Art Paper (Pinky Pig):

- Pink 12" x 18" (30.5 cm x 45.7 cm) head, neck, snout, hooves
- Blue 9" x 12" (22.9 cm x 30.5 cm) jacket
- Aluminum foil scrap for button

Art Paper (Giddy Goat):

- White 12" x 18" (30.5 cm x 45.7 cm) head, neck, scarf
- Gray 6" x 9" (15.2 cm x 22.9 cm) horns
- Black scrap for nose

Art Paper (Tommy Tortoise):

- Two green 9" x 12" (22.9 cm x 30.5 cm) head

Procedure

1. Follow directions on page 5 for tracing, cutting, and gluing head and cardboard neck strip. (Cover just the lower half of Tommy Tortoise's neck strip with green paper.)
2. Trace and cut out remaining pattern pieces.
3. Glue pieces in place (figs. A, B, and C).
4. Use a red marker or crayon to add stripes to Giddy Goat's scarf. Add other details with markers or crayons.

Figure A

Figure B

Figure C

Tales From Many Lands Papercrafts © 1991 Fearon Teacher Aids

head
pink

cut 2

place on fold

jacket
blue

place on fold

button

hooves
pink

cut 2

snout
pink

The Bojabi Tree (Pinky Pig Mask) 11

nose
black

scarf
white

place on fold

head
white

cut 2

horn
gray

cut 2

The Bojabi Tree (Giddy Goat Mask)

Tales From Many Lands Papercrafts © 1991 Fearon Teacher Aids

head
green

cut 2

place on fold

The Bojabi Tree (Tommy Tortoise Mask)

Oh, Kojo! How Could You! (Africa)

Oh, Kojo! How Could You! (River Spirit, Dog, and Cat Stick Puppets)

Materials

- Patterns on page 16 reproduced on white art paper
- White art paper 9" x 12" (22.9 cm x 30.5 cm)
- Tongue depressor or popsicle stick for each puppet

Procedure

1. Color patterns using crayons or markers.

2. Place white art paper behind pattern page and cut patterns out to produce two copies of each pattern. (Or patterns can be cut out and then traced and recut on the white art paper.)

3. Place a tongue depressor or popsicle stick between the patterns and glue the two pieces together. Allow the stick to extend enough to make a comfortable handle (figs. A, B, and C).

Figure A

Figure B

Figure C

River Spirit

Dog

Cat

Oh, Kojo! How Could You! (River Spirit, Dog, and Cat Stick Puppets)

Oh, Kojo! How Could You! (Kojo, Mother, and Ananse Stick Puppets)

Materials

- Patterns on page 18 reproduced on white art paper
- White art paper 9" x 12" (22.9 cm x 30.5 cm)
- Tongue depressor or popsicle stick for each puppet

Procedure

1. Color patterns using crayons or markers.

2. Place white art paper behind pattern page and cut patterns out to produce two copies of each pattern. (Or patterns can be cut out and then traced and recut on the white art paper.)

3. Place a tongue depressor or popsicle stick between the patterns and glue the two pieces together. Allow the stick to extend enough to make a comfortable handle (figs. A, B, and C).

Figure A

Figure B

Figure C

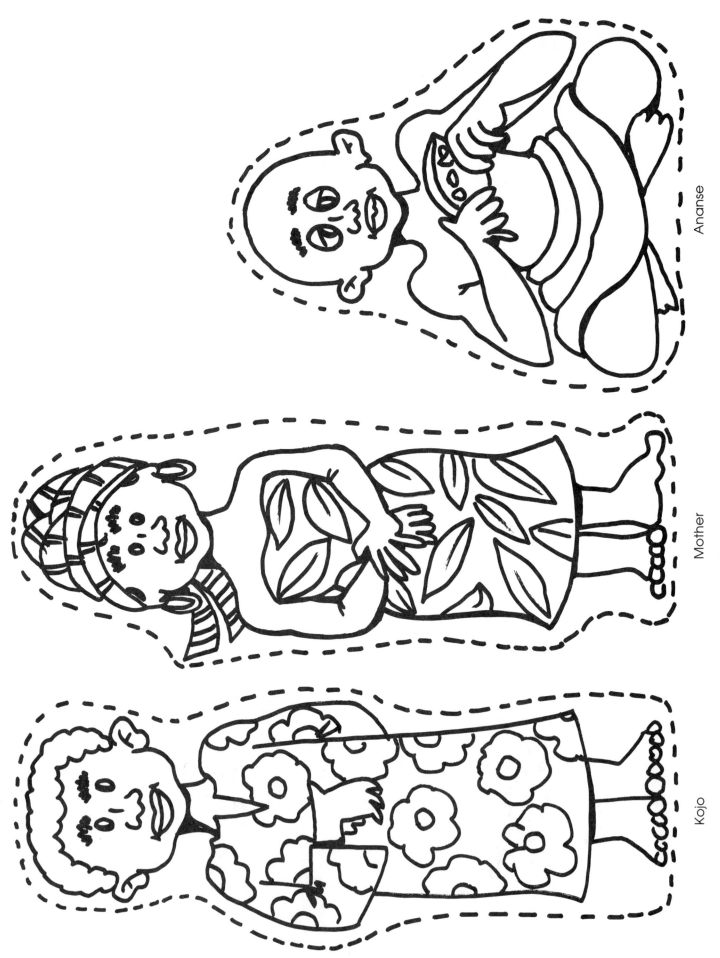

Ananse

Mother

Kojo

Oh, Kojo! How Could You! (Kojo, Mother, and Ananse Puppets)

Oh, Kojo! How Could You! (Dove)

Materials

- White art paper 12" x 18" (30.5 cm x 45.7 cm)
- Blue art paper strip 2" x 8" (5.0 cm x 20.3 cm)
- Stapler

Procedure

1. Trace and cut out dove pattern on white art paper.

2. Add details with markers or crayons.

3. Staple 2" x 8" (5.0 cm x 20.3 cm) strip into a cylinder-like shape.

4. Cut a 1/2" slit on each side of the cylinder (fig. A).

5. Glue the body portion of the dove together leaving the wings free.

6. Curl the wings by gently rolling them around a pencil so they arch outward.

7. Slide the bird between the slits in the cylinder (fig. B).

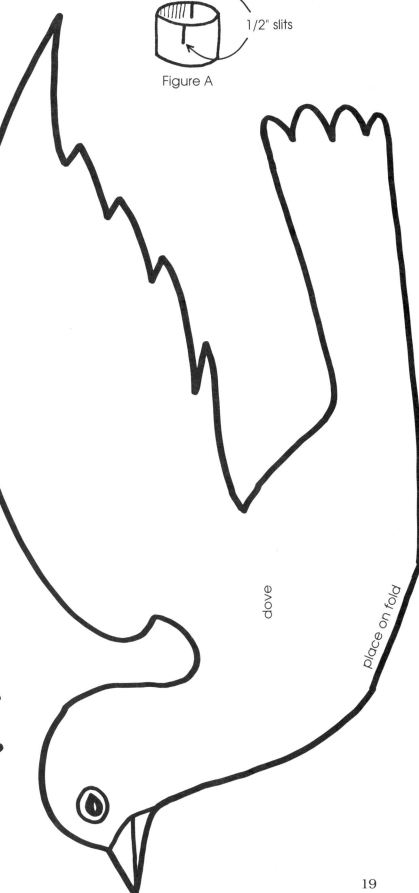

1/2" slits

Figure A

dove

place on fold

Figure B

Lon Po Po (China)

Tales From Many Lands Papercrafts © 1991 Fearon Teacher Aids

Lon Po Po (Shang, Tao, Paotze, and Mother Cylinder Puppets)

Materials

- Patterns on pages 22-23 reproduced on white art paper
- Stapler

Art Paper:
- Orange 9" x 12" (22.9 cm x 30.5 cm)
- Pink 9" x 12" (22.9 cm x 30.5 cm)
- Blue 9" x 12" (22.9 cm x 30.5 cm)
- Yellow 9" x 12" (22.9 cm x 30.5 cm)

Figure A

Procedure

1. Color the patterns with markers or crayons.

2. Cut out all pattern pieces.

3. Glue a body and head in the center of each colored 9" x 12" (22.9 cm x 30.5 cm) sheet of paper (fig. A).

4. Shape each sheet of colored paper into a cylinder and staple in the back at the top and bottom (figs. B, C, and D).

Figure B

Figure C

Figure D

Paotze's body

Tao's head

Paotze's head

Tao's body

Lon Po Po (Paotze and Tao Cylinder Puppets)

Shang's body

Shang's head

Mother

Lon Po Po (Shang and Mother Cylinder Puppets) 23

Lon Po Po (Wolf)

Materials

- Patterns on page 25 reproduced on brown art paper
- Berry basket (baskets that come with fruit sold at the grocery store work well)
- Pipe cleaners, string, or yarn
- Cotton balls or tissue

Procedure

1. Add details to the wolf patterns with markers or crayons.

2. Cut out both pattern pieces.

3. Place the two wolves back to back and glue the heads together. Spread apart the lower half of the wolves to form a stand (fig. A).

4. Attach pipe cleaners, string, or yarn to each corner of the berry basket.

5. Place wolf in basket and fill the basket with cotton balls or tissue to keep the wolf standing upright in the center (fig. B).

Figure A

Figure B

24

The Ugly Duckling (Denmark)

Tales From Many Lands Papercrafts © 1991 Fearon Teacher Aids

The Ugly Duckling

Materials

- Brass fastener

Art Paper:

- Yellow 9" x 12" (22.9 cm x 30.5 cm) shell
- Gray 6" x 9" (15.2 cm x 22.9 cm) duckling
- Black 2" x 2" (5.0 cm x 5.0 cm) beak, eye
- White scrap for eye

Procedure

1. Trace and cut out pattern pieces.

2. Glue eye and beak in place.

3. Glue duckling to bottom half of shell. (Be sure that when the top half of the shell is in place, the duckling does not stick up above the egg.)

4. Connect shell halves by sticking a brass fastener through the designated holes.

brass fastener

beak
black

eye
black and white
cut 1

shell
yellow

duckling
gray

shell
yellow

The Ugly Duckling

Tales From Many Lands Papercrafts © 1991 Fearon Teacher Aids

The Ugly Duckling (Swan Stick Puppet)

Materials

- Swan pattern (below) reproduced on white art paper
- White art paper 9" x 12" (22.9 cm x 30.5 cm)
- Tongue depressor or popsicle stick

Figure A

Procedure

1. Color pattern using crayons or markers.
2. Place white art paper behind pattern page and cut swan out. (Or pattern can be cut out and then traced and recut on the white art paper.)
3. Place a tongue depressor or popsicle stick between the two swans and glue the pieces together. Allow the stick to extend enough to make a comfortable handle (fig. A).

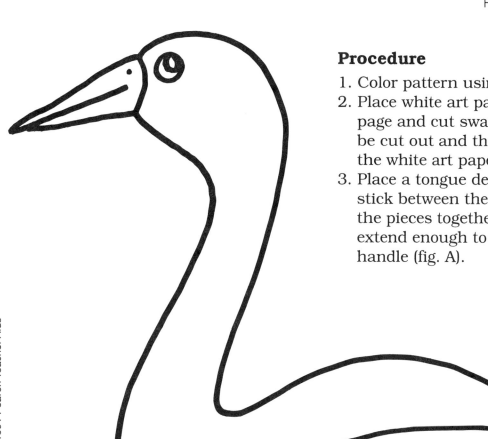

swan

cut 2

The Elves and the Shoemaker (Germany)

The Elves and the Shoemaker (Shoemaker, Wife, and Elf Jointed Puppets)

Materials

- Patterns on pages 32-33 reproduced on white art paper
- Tagboard
- Brass fasteners

Procedure

1. Color the pattern pieces with crayons or markers.
2. Cut out patterns. Patterns can be glued to tagboard first to give them more stability.
3. Stick brass fasteners through the designated holes to connect the pattern pieces (figs. A, B, and C).

Figure A

Figure B

Figure C

Shoemaker's body

Shoemaker's arms

Shoemaker's head

Wife's head

Wife's body

Wife's arms

Tales From Many Lands Papercrafts © 1991 Fearon Teacher Aids

32   **The Elves and the Shoemaker (Shoemaker and Wife Jointed Puppets)**

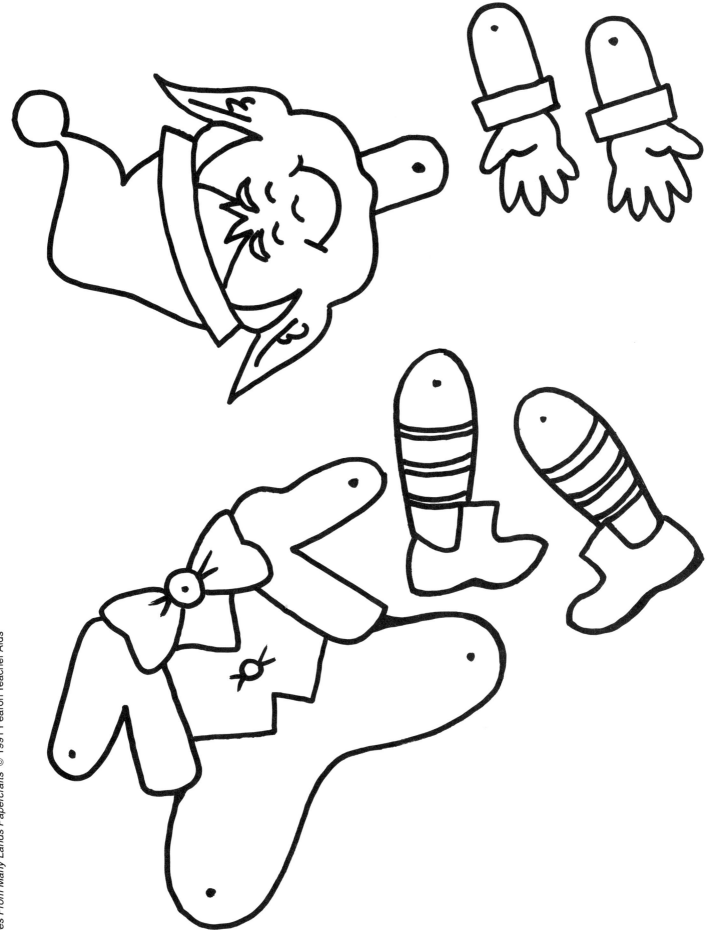

The Elves and the Shoemaker (Elf Jointed Puppet)   33

The Monkey and the Crocodile (India)

The Monkey and the Crocodile (Monkey and Crocodile Jointed Puppets)

Materials

- Brass fasteners

Art Paper (Monkey):

- Patterns on page 36 reproduced on brown art paper

Art Paper (Crocodile):

- Patterns on pages 37-38 reproduced on green art paper
- White art paper 2" x 5" (5.0 cm x 12.7 cm) for crocodile teeth

Procedure

1. Add details to the pattern pieces using crayons or markers.
2. Cut out patterns.
3. Retrace the crocodile teeth on white art paper. Glue the teeth in place on the crocodile jaw.
4. Stick brass fasteners through the designated holes to connect the pattern pieces (figs. A and B).

Figure A

Figure B

arms

upper arms

upper legs

lower legs

tail

The Monkey and the Crocodile (Monkey Jointed Puppet)

head

jaw

hind legs

front legs

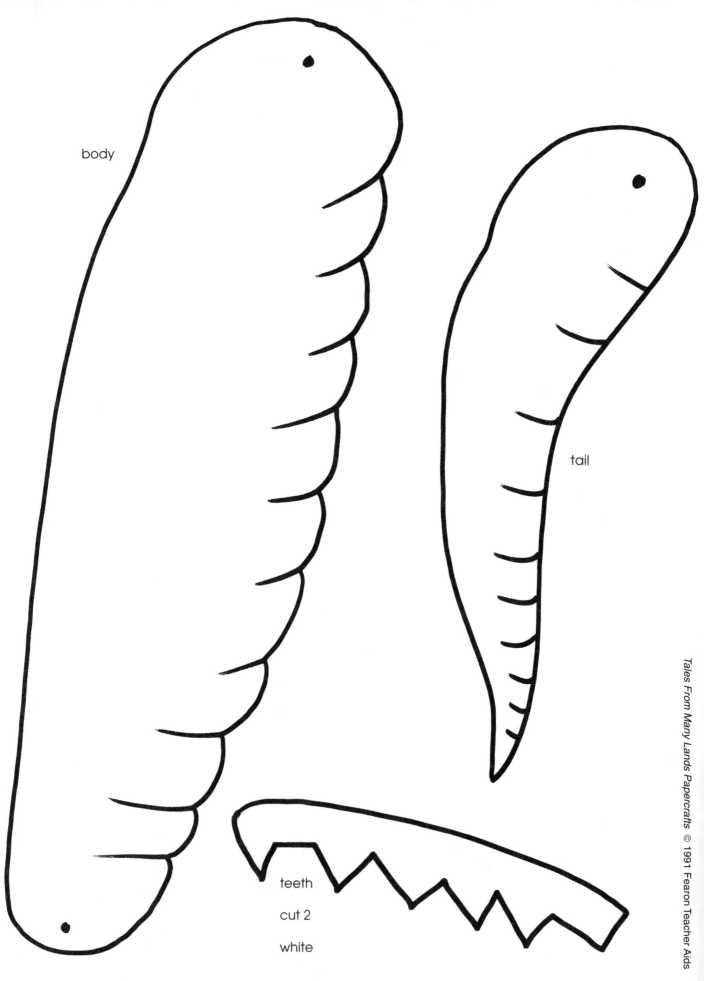

body

tail

teeth

cut 2

white

The Monkey and the Crocodile (Crocodile Jointed Puppet)

The Crane Wife (Japan)

The Crane Wife (Yohei, Wife, and Crane Stick Puppets)

Materials

- Patterns on pages 41-42 reproduced on white art paper
- Tongue depressor or popsicle stick for each puppet

Procedure

1. Color patterns using crayons or markers.
2. Place white art paper behind pattern page and cut patterns out to produce two copies of each pattern. (Or patterns can be cut out and then traced and recut on the white art paper.)
3. Place a tongue depressor or popsicle stick between the patterns and glue the two pieces together. Allow the stick to extend enough to make a comfortable handle (figs. A, B, and C).

Figure A

Figure B

Figure C

Tales From Many Lands Papercrafts © 1991 Fearon Teacher Aids

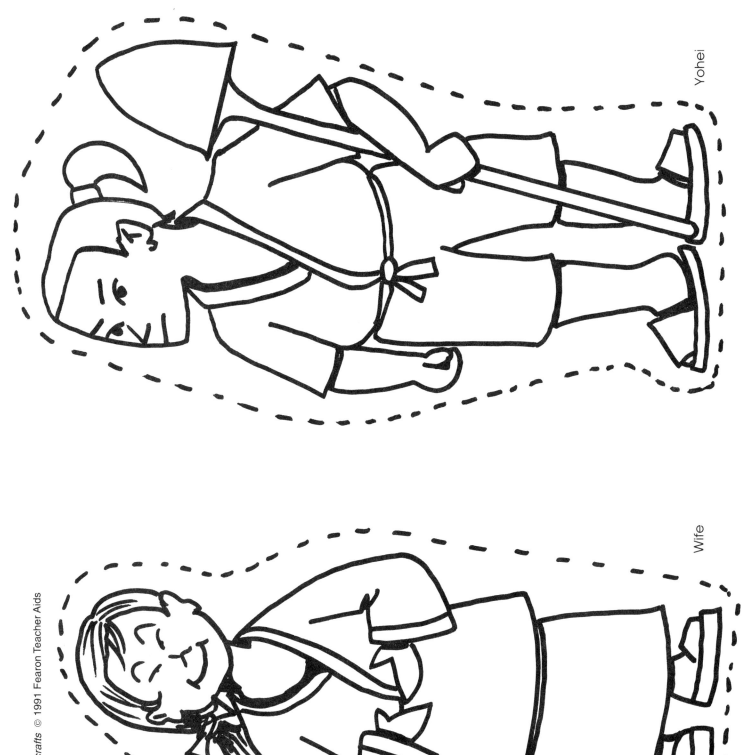

Yohei

Wife

The Crane Wife (Yohei and Wife Stick Puppets)   41

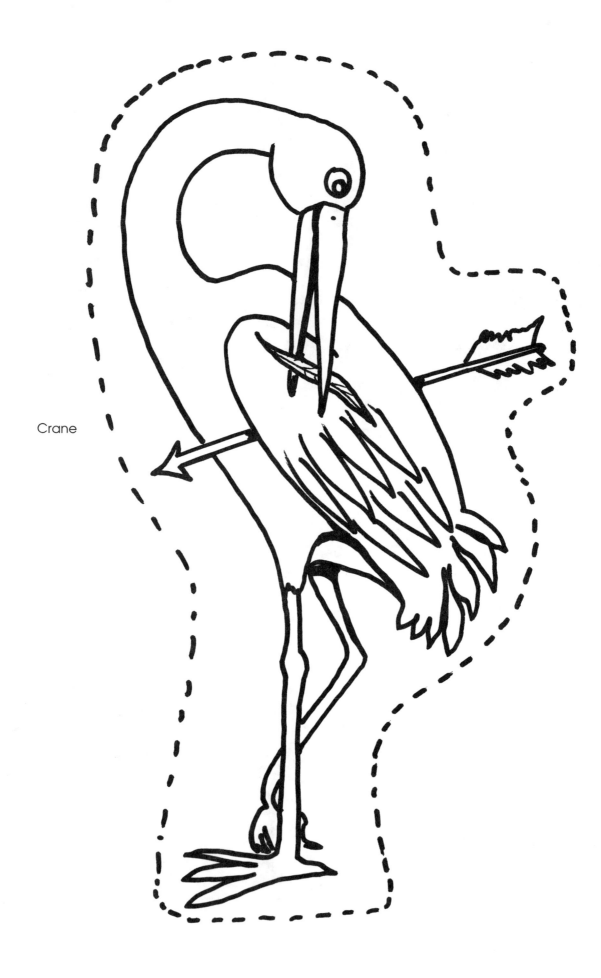

Crane

The Crane Wife (Crane Stick Puppet)

The Crane Wife (Feather Loom)

Materials

- Black marker or crayon
- Tape
- Purple art paper 9" x 12" (22.9 cm x 30.5 cm)
- Two black tagboard 9" x 12" (22.9 cm x 30.5 cm)

Procedure

1. Fold a 2" (5.0 cm) flap on one of the short ends of each sheet of black tagboard.
2. Fold one sheet of tagboard in half widthwise excluding the 2" (5.0 cm) flap.
3. Cut slits 1" (2.5 cm) apart starting at the folded end and stopping short of the 2" (5.0 cm) flap. Leave a 1/2" (1.3 cm) border on each side and a 1" (2.5 cm) border on the top (fig. A). Unfold (fig B). (If you use heavyweight tagboard, cut slits with an X-acto knife.)
4. Cut out the feather pattern. Trace and cut out six feathers from the purple paper. (Fold purple paper in half widthwise and then into thirds lengthwise before tracing to cut all six feathers at once.)
5. Use a black marker to add details to the feathers.
6. Weave the feathers through the slits in the black tagboard and glue the ends in place.
7. Use tape to attach the two pieces of black tagboard at the ends without the folded flaps.
8. Glue the folded flaps together to make the loom stand by itself (fig. C).

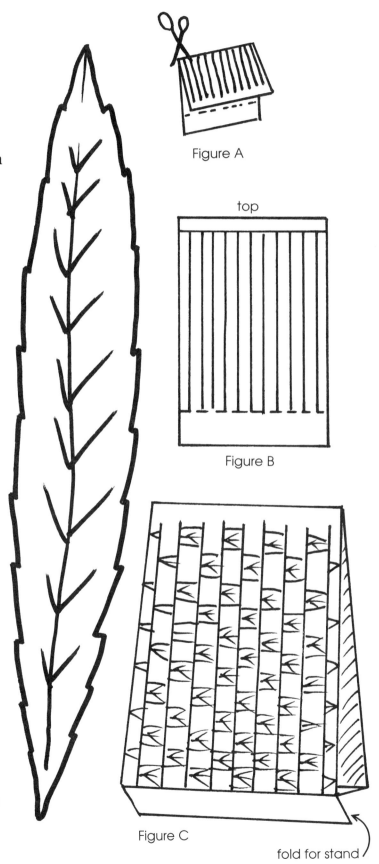

Figure A

top

Figure B

Figure C

fold for stand

The Whale in the Sky (Native American)

The Whale in the Sky (Totem Pole)

Materials

- Patterns on pages 46-47 reproduced on white art paper
- Black art paper 12" x 18" (30.5 cm x 45.7 cm)
- Stapler
- Tape

Procedure

1. Color patterns with markers or crayons.

2. Cut out patterns.

3. Lay the black paper lengthwise on a table or desk and glue the frog at the base in the center. Glue the rest of the animals in order from bottom to top to create a totem pole (salmon, raven, whale, thunderbird). The thunderbird will stick up above the edge of the black paper (fig. A).

4. Fold the black paper into a long cylinder and staple at the top and bottom. Use tape to keep the edges in the center of the totem pole together.

Figure A

Thunderbird

Salmon

46   **The Whale in the Sky (Totem Pole)**

Tales From Many Lands Papercrafts © 1991 Fearon Teacher Aids

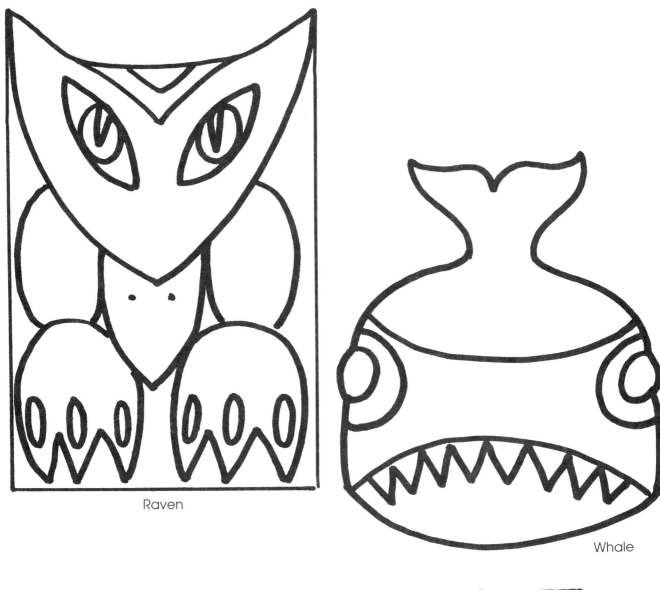

Raven

Whale

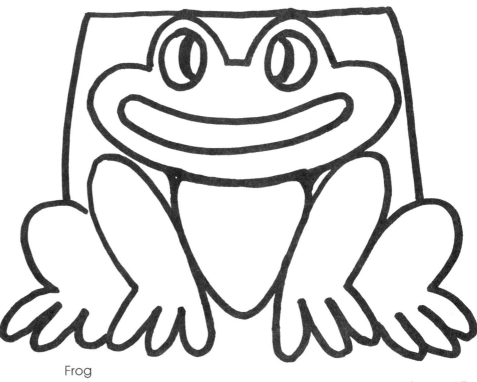

Frog

Tales From Many Lands Papercrafts © 1991 Fearon Teacher Aids

The Whale in the Sky (Totem Pole)   47

The Lad and the North Wind (Norway)

The Lad and the North Wind (Ram Puppet)

Materials

- Two plastic eyes
- Tongue depressor or popsicle stick

Art Paper:

- Black
  9" x 12" (22.9 cm x 30.5 cm) body
  9" x 12" (22.9 cm x 30.5 cm) head

- White 4" x 9" (10.2 cm x 22.9 cm) face, hooves

- Pink scrap for nose

- Gray scrap for goatee

Procedure

1. To make ram body, fold black 9" x 12" (22.9 cm x 30.5 cm) paper in half widthwise (fig. A).

2. Cut in 2" (5.0 cm) from the top on each side (fig. B).

3. Fold flaps inside (fig. C).

4. Cut neck hole (fig. D).

5. Trace and cut out pattern pieces.

6. Glue tongue depressor or popsicle stick between the two head patterns allowing half of the stick to extend.

7. Glue remaining pieces in place (fig. E).

8. Place neck inside hole cut in body and glue in place.

9. Add details with markers or crayons.

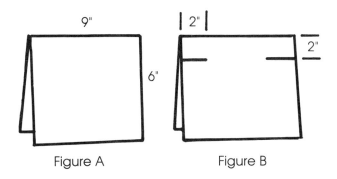

Figure A   Figure B

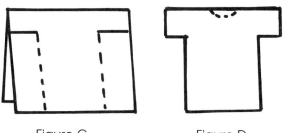

Figure C   Figure D

Figure E

nose
pink

ram face
white

ram head
black

cut 2

place on fold

wind cloud
white

cut 2

goatee
gray

ram hoof
white

cut 2

The Lad and the North Wind (Ram and Wind Puppets)

The Lad and the North Wind (Wind Stick Puppet)

Materials

- Tongue depressor or popsicle stick
- White art paper 9" x 12" (22.9 cm x 30.5 cm)

Procedure

1. Trace and cut out pattern on white art paper.

2. Add details with markers or crayons.

3. Place a tongue depressor or popsicle stick between the patterns and glue the two pieces together. Allow the stick to extend enough to make a comfortable handle (fig. A).

Figure A

The Lad and the North Wind
(Peter Puppet)

Materials

- Tongue depressor or popsicle stick
- Two plastic eyes

Art Paper:

- Blue 6" x 9" (15.2 cm x 22.9 cm) coveralls
- Yellow 6" x 9" (15.2 cm x 22.9 cm) shirt
- Pink or brown 6" x 9" (15.2 cm x 22.9 cm) head, ears, hands
- Black 4" x 9" (10.2 cm x 22.9 cm) hair
- Black scraps for shoes

Procedure

1. Trace and cut out all pattern pieces.

2. Glue tongue depressor or popsicle stick between the two head patterns allowing half of the stick to extend. Glue hair and plastic eyes in place and add details with markers or crayons (fig. A).

3. Fold shirt where indicated by dotted line and cut neck hole (fig. B).

4. Glue remaining pattern pieces in place (fig. C).

5. Place stick into the neck hole and glue to the back shirt flap. Manipulate puppet by holding the extended portion of the tongue depressor or popsicle stick (fig. D).

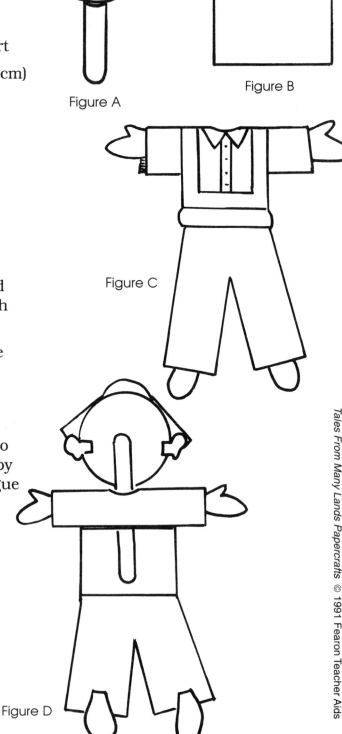

Figure A

Figure B

Figure C

Figure D

Tales From Many Lands Papercrafts © 1991 Fearon Teacher Aids

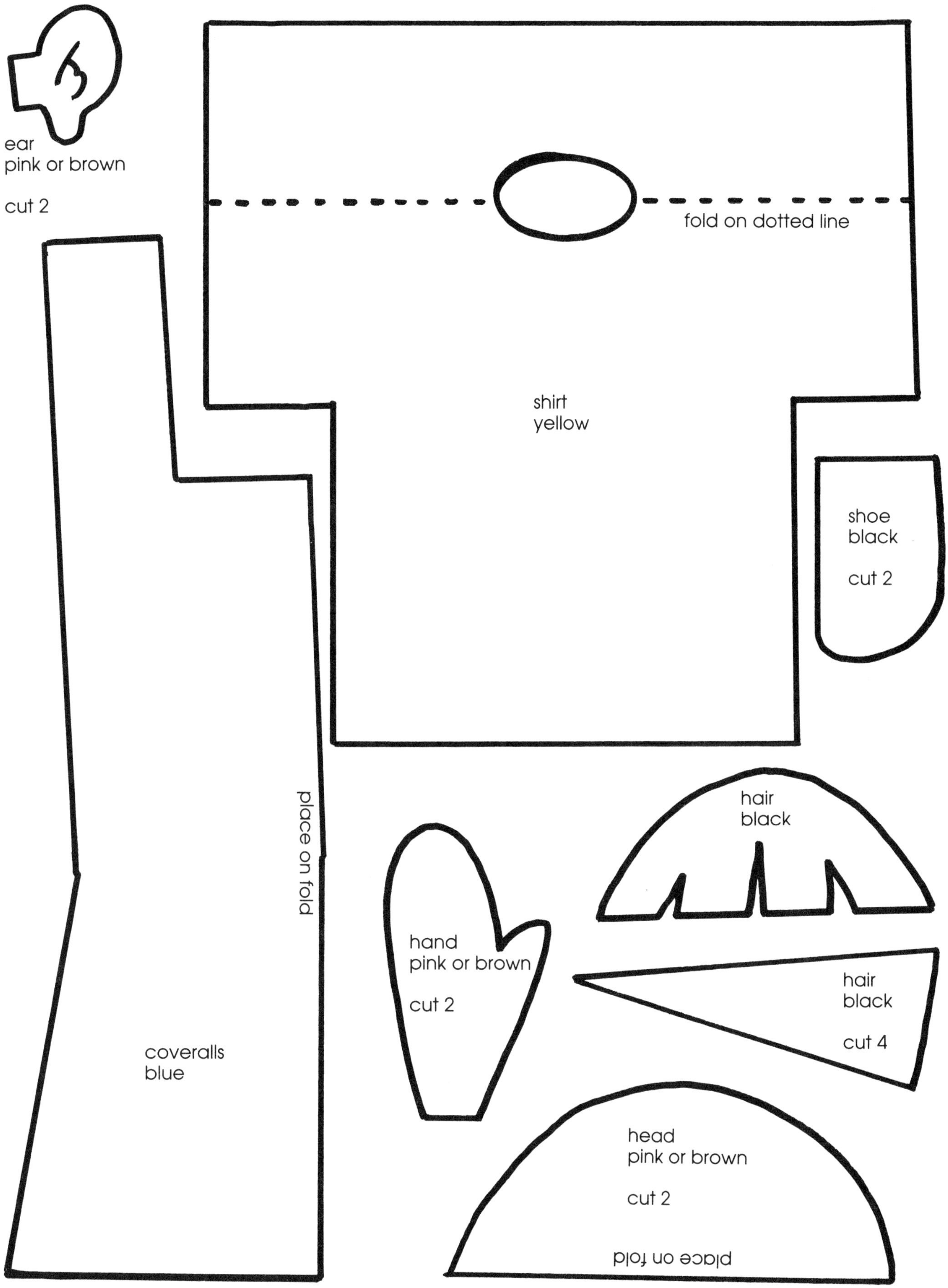

ear
pink or brown

cut 2

fold on dotted line

shirt
yellow

shoe
black

cut 2

place on fold

coveralls
blue

hand
pink or brown

cut 2

hair
black

hair
black

cut 4

head
pink or brown

cut 2

place on fold

The Lad and the North Wind (Mother and Innkeeper Puppets)

Materials
- Tongue depressor or popsicle stick for each puppet
- Two plastic eyes for each puppet

Art Paper (Mother):
- Green 6" x 9" (15.2 cm x 22.9 cm) shirt
- Pink or brown 6" x 9" (15.2 cm x 22.9 cm) face, hands
- Black 4" x 6" (10.2 cm x 15.2 cm) skirt
- White 6" x 9" (15.2 cm x 22.9 cm) hair, apron, collar
- Brown scrap for shoes

Art Paper (Innkeeper):
- Light blue 6" x 9" (15.2 cm x 22.9 cm) shirt
- Dark blue 4" x 6" (10.2 cm x 15.2 cm) trousers
- Pink or brown 6" x 9" (15.2 cm x 22.9 cm) face, hands, ears
- White 6" x 9" (15.2 cm x 22.9 cm) apron
- Black scrap for shoes and bow tie
- Gray scrap for hair

Procedure
1. Trace and cut out all pattern pieces.

2. Glue tongue depressor or popsicle stick between the two head patterns allowing half of the stick to extend. Glue hair and plastic eyes in place and add details with markers or crayons.

3. Fold shirt where indicated by dotted line and cut neck hole.

4. Glue remaining pattern pieces in place (figs. A and B).

5. Place stick into the neck hole and glue to the back shirt flap. Manipulate puppet by holding the extended portion of the tongue depressor or popsicle stick.

Figure A

Figure B

Tales From Many Lands Papercrafts © 1991 Fearon Teacher Aids

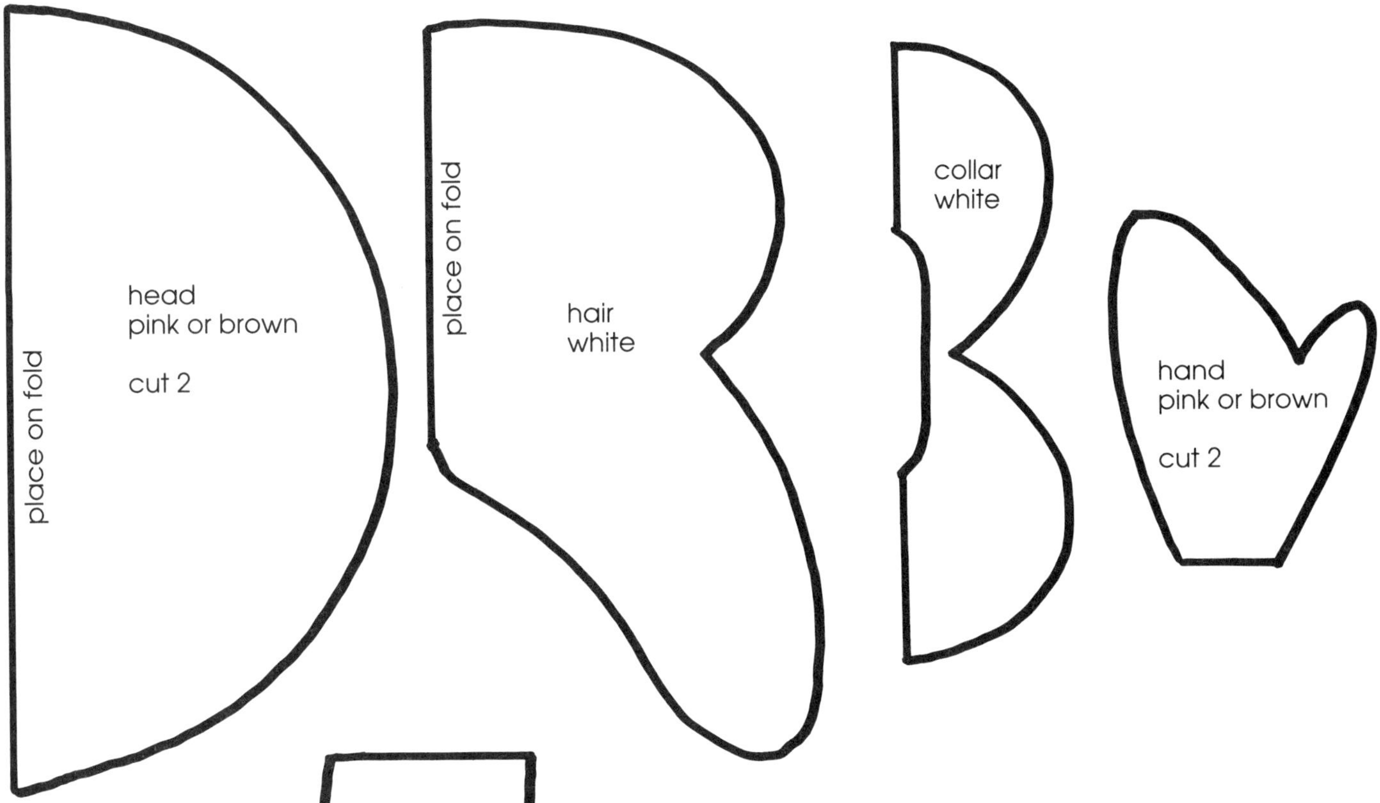

head
pink or brown

cut 2

place on fold

place on fold

hair
white

collar
white

hand
pink or brown

cut 2

shoe
brown

cut 2

Use shirt pattern on
page 53. Trace and
cut on green paper.

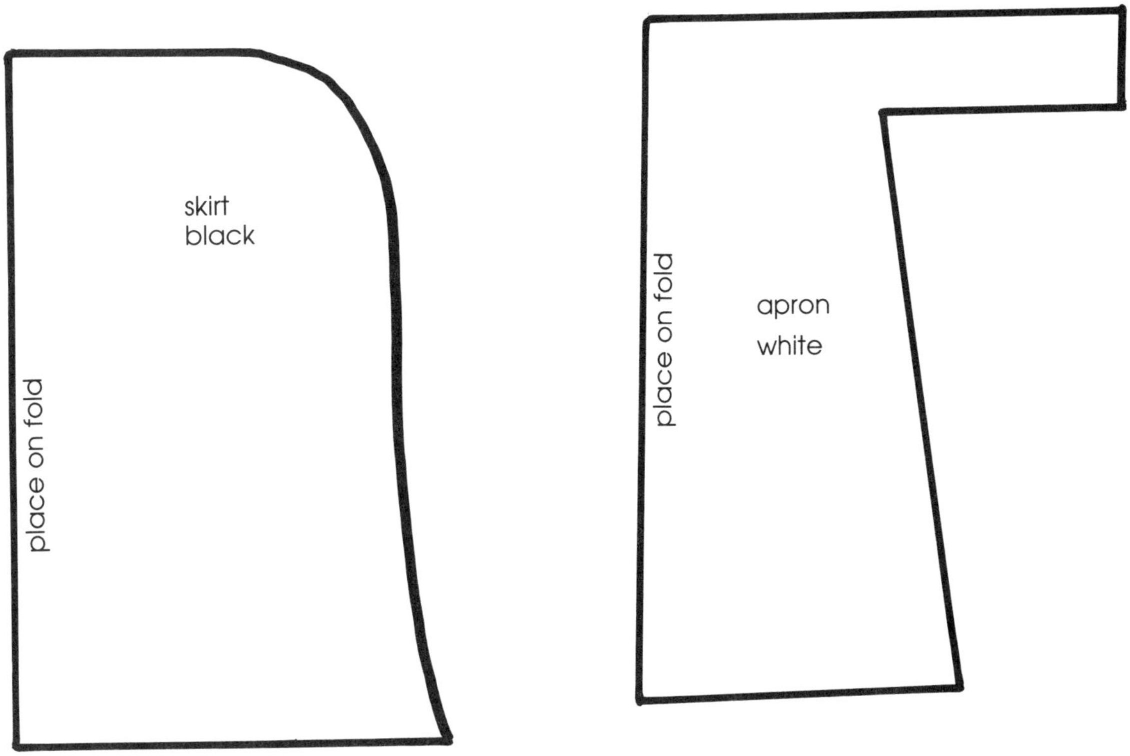

skirt
black

place on fold

place on fold

apron
white

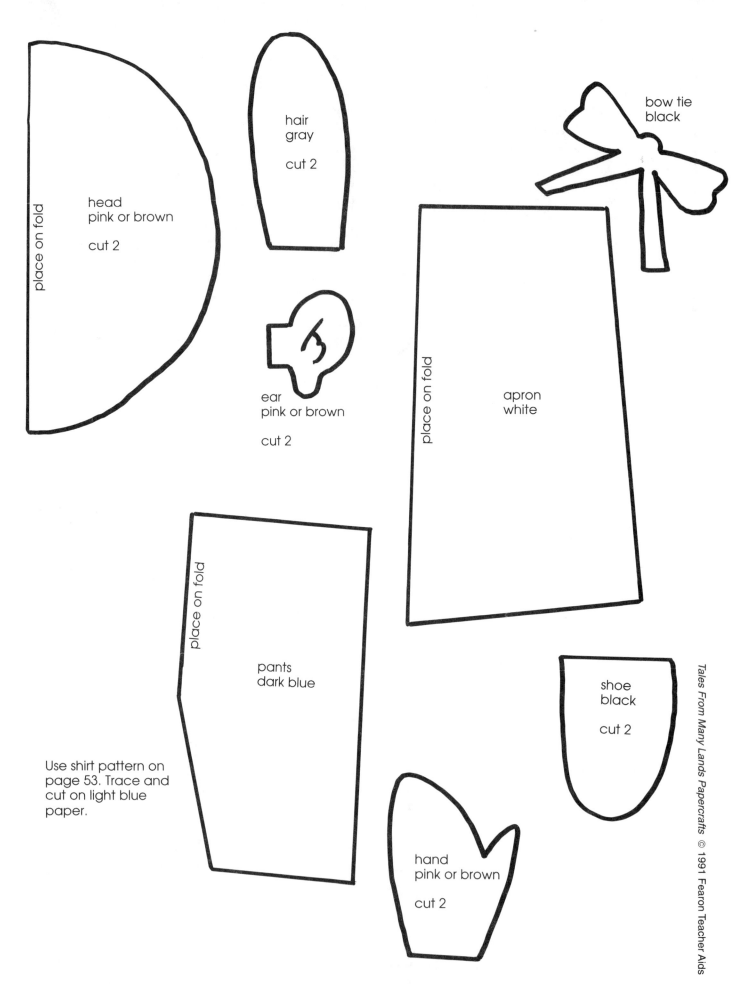

place on fold

head
pink or brown

cut 2

hair
gray

cut 2

bow tie
black

ear
pink or brown

cut 2

place on fold

apron
white

place on fold

pants
dark blue

Use shirt pattern on page 53. Trace and cut on light blue paper.

shoe
black

cut 2

hand
pink or brown

cut 2

Tales From Many Lands Papercrafts © 1991 Fearon Teacher Aids

The Lad and the North Wind (Innkeeper Puppet)

The Straw Ox (Russia)

The Straw Ox (Ox, Man, Woman, Bear, Rabbit, Wolf, and Fox Puppets)

Materials

- Tagboard strip 2" x 18" (5.0 cm x 45.7 cm) for each puppet
- String, yarn or thread 24" (61 cm) for each puppet
- Hole punch
- Patterns on pages 59-63 reproduced on art paper listed below

Art Paper:
- Yellow 9" x 12" (22.9 cm x 30.5 cm) Straw Ox
- White 9" x 12" (22.9 cm x 30.5 cm) Man
- White 9" x 12" (22.9 cm x 30.5 cm) Woman
- Brown 9" x 12" (22.9 cm x 30.5 cm) Bear
- White 9" x 12" (22.9 cm x 30.5 cm) Rabbit
- Gray 9" x 12" (22.9 cm x 30.5 cm) Wolf
- Red 9" x 12" (22.9 cm x 30.5 cm) Fox

Figure B

Figure C

Procedure

1. Color figure and add details with markers or crayons.

2. Cut figure out.

3. Fold the tagboard strip in half and fold each end up 2" (5.0 cm) to create tabs (fig. A).

4. Overlap the 2" (5.0 cm) tabs and glue them together to make a triangular stand (fig. B).

5. Punch a hole at the top of the triangle and tie the string through the hole.

6. Glue figure to one side of triangle (figs. C and D).

7. Hold string to manipulate puppet. (For more control, glue a small rock or other weight inside the bottom of the triangular stand.)

Figure D

Tales From Many Lands Papercrafts © 1991 Fearon Teacher Aids

2"   • •   2"

Figure A

The Straw Ox (Ox Puppet) 59

The Straw Ox (Man Puppet)

Tales From Many Lands Papercrafts © 1991 Fearon Teacher Aids

The Straw Ox (Woman Puppet)   61

The Straw Ox (Bear and Rabbit Puppets)

Wolf

Fox

The Straw Ox (Puppet Theatre)

Materials

- Cardboard box
- Assorted colors and sizes of art paper

Procedure

1. Cut away one side of an open cardboard box (fig. A)

2. Design scenery using art paper and glue it in place.

3. Puppet operators stand behind the box to manipulate puppets.

Figure A

Tales From Many Lands Papercrafts © 1991 Fearon Teacher Aids